Enid Blyton's

THE FLYAWAY
BROOMSTICK

and other stories

CLIVEDEN PRESS

Published in Great Britain in 1994 by Cliveden Press,
an imprint of Egmont Publishing Limited, Egmont House,
PO Box 111, Great Ducie Street, Manchester M60 3BL.
Printed in Finland

ISBN 0 7498 2038 1

Enid Blyton

Enid Blyton was born in London in 1897. Her childhood was spent in Beckenham, Kent, and as a child she began to write poems, stories and plays. She trained to be a teacher but she devoted her whole life to being a children's author. Her first book was a collection of poems for children, published in 1922. In 1926 she began to write a weekly magazine for children called *Sunny Stories*, and it was here that many of her most popular stories and characters first appeared. The magazine was immensely popular and in 1953 it became *The Enid Blyton Magazine*.

She wrote more than 600 books for children and many of her most popular series are still published all over the world. Her books have been translated into over 30 languages. Enid Blyton died in 1968.

Contents

The swallow fairy

Once there was a small fairy who played all summer long with the swallows. She had long curved wings as they had, and she flashed in the air with them, racing them over the fields and back.

They lived on the insects they caught in the air. The swallow fairy lived on the nectar she found in the flowers. The bees and butterflies showed her how to get it with a long, very tiny spoon.

"We have a tongue to put into the flowers, to suck out the nectar," they said, "but you haven't a long enough one. So use a spoon."

Now, in October, a cold wind blew. The swallow fairy shivered. There were not so many flowers with honey in and she was sometimes hungry.

There were not so many insects flying in the air either, so the swallows were often hungry. And when the cold wind blew, they gathered together on the roofs of barns and on the telegraph wires, chattering and twittering.

The little martins were there with the swallows, too. They were cousins of the swallows, and loved to fly with them high in the sky. "Don't let's stay here in this cold wind!" they cried. "Let's fly off to a warmer country."

"Yes, do let's!" said the swallows. "In a warmer country there will be more insects. There are so few here now. We will go!"

"Oh, don't leave me!" cried the swallow fairy. "I shall be so lonely. Take me with you."

"It's too far for you to fly," said her best friend, a fine long-tailed swallow with a shining steel-blue back. "You would fall into the sea and be drowned."

"Oh, will you fly across the sea?" said the fairy. "I shouldn't like that. I'll stay here – but you will come back again?"

"In the springtime," said the swallow, and then suddenly, almost as if one of them had given a signal, the whole twittering flock flew into the air and wheeled away to the south. They were gone. Not one was left.

The fairy was lonely. She sat crying in the evening wind, sitting on a barn roof by herself. A little black bat saw her and flew near.

"Come and live with me!" he cried. "Do come!"

So the fairy went to live with him. But as the wind grew colder he wouldn't go out to fly. He hung himself upside down in an old cave, with hundreds of others like himself. And he went to sleep!

"Wake up, wake up!" cried the fairy. "You're a dull sort of friend to have, little bat!"

"Leave me alone," said the bat, sleepily. "I'm too cold to fly. I shall sleep

9

till the sun comes again in the spring. Hang yourself upside down, fairy, and sleep, too."

"I don't like hanging upside down," said the fairy. "I don't like hanging myself up at all. And I don't like this cave, either. It smells."

"Well, go and live with someone else then," said the bat, in a huff, and he wouldn't say another word.

The fairy flew off. She came to a pond and sat by it, feeling cold and lonely. A frog was there, talking to a fat, squat toad.

"Hallo, fairy!" said the frog. "Why do you look so miserable?"

"I'm lonely," said the fairy. "I've no friend to live with."

"You'd better tuck yourself away somewhere for the winter," said the frog. "Come with me and I'll keep you close to me, little fairy."

"All right," said the fairy. "Where are you going?"

"I'm going down into the mud at the

bottom of the pond," said the frog. "I shall sleep there all the winter. It's a nice cosy place to sleep."

"Oh, I'd *hate* that!" said the fairy and shivered. "Cold and muddy and wet! I'd rather go with the toad. I always did like his lovely brown eyes."

"Yes, you come with me," said the toad, and took her to a big stone. Underneath was a fine hiding-place, just big enough for the fairy and himself. He dragged her underneath with him. Then he shut his eyes. The fairy went to sleep, too. But she soon awoke and shivered.

"This is a nasty damp place," she said. "I shall get a cold. Toad, let's go somewhere else?"

But the toad was fast asleep and wouldn't answer. So the fairy left him in disgust. She walked fast to keep herself warm – and ran into a hedgehog, also hurrying fast. He carried a leaf in his mouth.

"Oh, hullo!" said the fairy. "Where are

you off to, with that leaf?"

"I've got a cosy little house in a warm bank," said the hedgehog. "I'm lining it with leaves. Why don't you come and live with me there? It's really a very nice little home, with a curtain of moss for a door."

"All right, I'll come," said the fairy, who thought the hedgehog's home sounded nice. It *was* nice, too, all lined with dry dead leaves, and quite warm.

But the hedgehog was so prickly that the fairy couldn't possibly cuddle up to him. And whenever he moved, his prickles stuck into her. That wasn't at all nice.

"I'll have to go," said the fairy. "I'm sorry, but you're not very cuddly, hedgehog."

The hedgehog said nothing. He was fast asleep. He wouldn't wake up for weeks!

"This is very boring," said the fairy to herself, scrambling out of the warm hole. "All my friends seem either to be flying off to warmer lands, or finding places to sleep away the winter. I don't want to do either, but I *must* find somewhere for a home. And I'd dearly like to have a nice friend I could talk to, too, not one who's going to snore all winter long."

She met a snake, and he invited her to go to a hollow tree he knew and curl up with him and all his friends together. "We knot ourselves together for warmth." he said. "It's an awfully nice tree we go to, fairy. Do come."

"Well – no, thank you," said the fairy. "I like snakes and I think they're very clever the way they glide along without feet – but I don't want to be knotted up with you all winter. I might want to get out and not be able to, because I'm sure you'd all be fast asleep."

"Oh, we should," said the snake. "Well, what about trying the dormouse? He's a nice cosy fellow, and he would keep you warm and not mind a bit if you wriggled in and out of his hole during the winter. He's in the ditch over there."

The dormouse was very fat. He told the fairy that as he never had anything to eat all the winter, he liked to get as nice and fat as possible before he went to sleep.

"Don't you ever wake up in the winter?" said the fairy. "I really do want a cosy, furry friend like you to cuddle up to, but it's so dull having a friend who is asleep all the time and never says a word. And oh dear! I don't know *what* I shall do for food soon. There isn't any nectar to be found at all, except in a few odd flowers here and there."

The dormouse went close to her and whispered, "I know where there is a store of nuts. Do you like nuts?"

"Oh, yes," said the fairy. "Very much."

"Well, do you see that clump of ivy over there?" asked the dormouse, pointing with his tiny foot. "I happen to know there are about a dozen nuts there. You could feast on those."

"Oh, thank you," said the fairy. She watched the dormouse go down to his little hole in some tree-roots. She liked him very much – but he *would* be dull as a friend, because she knew what a sleepy fellow he was.

She flew to the ivy and found the nuts. She was just wondering how to crack one when she heard a cross voice: "Hey! Don't take my nuts!"

"Oh – are they yours? I'm so sorry," said the fairy, and put the nut back quickly. She looked at the animal beside her. She liked him very much. He was a red squirrel, with bright eyes and a very bushy tail.

The squirrel looked at the fairy, and he liked her, too. He was suddenly sorry he had been cross, because the fairy looked cold and hungry and lonely. He took up a nut. "Would you like me to give you one?" he said. "I don't like people to steal them, but I never mind giving them away."

He gnawed through the shell, and got out the nut. He gave it to the fairy. "Oh, thank you," she said, and began to nibble it.

"You seem very hungry," said the squirrel. "Where is your home?"

"I haven't one," said the fairy, and she told him how she had tried to find someone to live with in warmth and friendliness. "You see – so many creatures go to sleep all the winter – and that's dull, isn't it?"

"Very dull," agreed the squirrel. "I think what *I* do is much more sensible. I sleep in my cosy hole when the weather is very bitter, with my tail wrapped round me for a rug – and when a warm spell comes, I wake up, scamper down my tree and find my nuts to have a feast. I have a good play, and then when the frosty night comes again, I pop back to sleep."

"That does sound a good idea," said the fairy. "Sleep the coldest days away – wake up in the sunshine and play, and have a good meal – and go back again when the frost nips your toes. You're the most sensible of all the creatures I know, Squirrel. How I wish you were my friend!"

"I'd like to be," said the squirrel. "You come with me to my hole and sleep with me, wrapped up in my tail. And perhaps, in the springtime, when I want to go and find a nice little wife, you'd brush and comb my fur well, and make me beautiful."

"Oh, I *will*!" said the fairy. "I'd love to do that."

So up the tree they went, and the squirrel curled up in his hole with the fairy beside him. He wrapped his bushy tail round them both, and they slept cosily together.

And when a warm spell comes they both wake up and look for the squirrel's nuts. So, if ever you see a red squirrel scampering in the winter sunshine, look around and see if you can spy his small companion hiding anywhere.

One moonlight night

The big round moon shone in at the playroom window, and the toys looked up at it in delight.

"It's so nice to have a lamp shining in the sky tonight," said the pink rabbit. "We can see what we are doing! Shall we play hide-and-seek?"

"No. Let's have a ride in the wooden train," said the teddy bear. "Come on."

"But where *is* it?" said the clockwork clown, looking round in surprise. "It's not here!"

"Good gracious! Where's it gone?" said the little golden-haired doll.

"*I* know!" cried the clockwork mouse. "Don't you remember – the two children took it out to let it run down the garden path, carrying the two little kittens? They must have left it out in the garden."

"Let's go and get it," said the clockwork clown, who enjoyed a bit of an adventure. "Come on – we can all climb out of the window!"

So out they climbed, and slid down the creeper growing up the wall. They set off to the garden path where they had last seen the wooden train. Yes – there it was, with its long line of little wooden carriages.

Well, the toys played round the train for a little while, and then suddenly they stopped.

They all listened – and sure enough it was a little voice from down the garden, shouting loudly.

"Help! Oh, please help!" came the shouts again. "H – ELLLLLL – PPPPP!"

"Good gracious!" puffed the engine. "We'd better go and see what's happening. That sounds like the little family of pixies who live down the old rabbit hole. They're so nice. Who'll come with me to rescue them?"

"I'm too little," said the clockwork mouse.

"I'm too fat," said the teddy bear.

"I'm too frightened," said the golden-haired doll.

"My clockwork's run down," said the clockwork clown.

"Well, dear me – I'm the only one left to go!" said the pink rabbit. "I don't want to – I'm scared. But I suppose I must."

"Of course you must," puffed the engine. "Get into my cab and drive me. Go on – quickly!"

The pink rabbit climbed into the cab and drove the train down the garden path – bumpity-bumpity-bump! He came to the end of it and ran the train over the lawn. Soon they arrived at the hedge where the rabbit hole was – and will you believe it, those wicked little red imps, no bigger than fieldmice, had caught all the pretty little pixies and tied them up!

"Listen," puffed the engine quietly, "tell the red imps I'll give them a ride round the garden for a treat. You stay here with the pixies, and undo their ropes."

"No," said the pink rabbit angrily. "I won't have you giving those bad red imps a treat like that."

"Do as you're told," said the engine, puffing so hard that the pink rabbit fell over.

He went to the red imps sulkily. "The engine says it will give you a ride round the garden if you like," he said.

"Oooooh! Come on, then!" cried the biggest imp, and ran to the carriages. "I've always wanted a ride in a train. Don't you try to untie those pixies, Rabbit – if you do, we'll tie *you* up, and throw you into a prickly rose bush!"

They were soon sitting in the wooden carriages of the little train. What fun! The imps leaned over the sides and laughed excitedly. A ride in a train! Well, what a surprise! The biggest one called out to the frightened pixies.

"You stay there till we come back. You can't run far, anyway!"

Rumble-rumble-rumble! Away went the wooden train round the garden, the imps squeaking in delight. The pink rabbit frowned after it. "Horrid train – being so nice to the bad red imps! Well – I must try and undo these knots, and set the poor little pixies free. But I *am* so bad at knots!"

"Just undo *mine*," said a small pixie with a silvery dress that shone in the moonlight. "Then I can undo all the others. My fingers are small, you see – yours are so large and clumsy, Rabbit. Just undo *my* knots! Hurry!"

"Good idea," said the pink rabbit, and began to undo the knots that tied up the little pixie. His fingers were large and the knots were small – but at last he had them all undone, and the pixie gave a cry of delight.

"Good! Thank you very much. Now I'll undo the others. Oh dear, I do hope

the train doesn't come back yet! I don't want to be tied up all over again!"

She ran to her friends, and tugged at their knots – and then, alas, the pink rabbit heard the train puffing back again!

"Ha-ha-ha!" it puffed. "He-he-he! Ho-ho-ho!"

"It sounds as if it's laughing," said the pink rabbit, in disgust. "Surely it isn't happy because it's taking those horrid red imps for a ride!"

The wooden train ran up, bumpity-bump, still chuckling. Well, what a surprise – all the carriages were empty!

"Where are those imps?" asked the pink rabbit, astonished.

"Well, you didn't *really* think I was being kind and giving those red imps a treat, did you?" said the engine. "Of course not! I ran them down the garden path, straight to the little pond. And then I ran right into the water, and in they fell with such a splash! *I* floated, of course, because I'm wooden, and I soon got out again – but the imps are still there!"

"What – in the pond?" cried the rabbit in delight.

"Yes. Some are sitting shivering on the lily-leaves, some are being chased by a big frog, and the others are spluttering and yelling!" said the engine, giving a sudden giggle. "But they'll soon find their way out of the water – so for goodness sake tell the pixies to get into my carriages, and I'll take them safely to the playroom at once. They can spend the night in the dolls' house."

The pixies climbed up the creeper with the pink rabbit to help them. The teddy bear and the others were there to help too. They made a great fuss of the pink rabbit who really felt quite a hero!

And now the tiny pixies are all fast asleep in the dolls' house very comfortable indeed. The pink rabbit has locked the door, in case the red imps come back.

But they won't. They've all gone

home, wet through, to dry their clothes! "Oh that rabbit!" said the biggest one. "Telling us to have a ride in that horrid train. Just wait till we meet him again! We'll soon find those pixies and tie them up even more tightly!"

But they won't find them, because a strange thing has happened. The pink rabbit has lost the key to the front door of the dolls' house! So the pixies can't get out and are still living there happily, very, very pleased to have such a nice home!

But I can't think what Jean and Donald will say when they play with the dolls' house next week – and see the little pixie family living so happily in its four small rooms!

The castle without a door

Once upon a time a wizard came to live just outside Brownie Town. He was called Kookle, and no one knew much about him.

"He's building himself a castle on the hill," they said to one another. "He just sits on a stone and says strange words, and the castle grows out of the ground. It is wonderful to watch."

"But it's a very strange castle," said Tinker, a fat jolly brownie. "Do you know that it hasn't any doors at all? How are people going to get in and out? That's what I'd like to know. The windows are far too high up to climb through."

"That's very funny," said the

brownies, and they shook their heads. "Perhaps Kookle is up to mischief of some sort."

It wasn't long before Kookle was very much disliked. He never spoke to the brownies at all, not even when they wished him good day. He turned one of them into a pillarbox one day because the little brownie had accidentally run into him round a corner, and it took Brownie Town a whole week before they could find the right magic to turn the pillarbox back into a brownie.

"He is a horrid wizard," said the little folk. "If only we could get rid of him! But what can you do with someone who lives in a castle without any doors? You can't even get in!"

"He'll do worse mischief yet, you mark my words!" said Tinker.

Now two weeks after that, little Princess Peronel came to stay in Brownie Town with her old nurse, Mother Browneyes. They went walking in Wishing Wood every day.

Then one day a dreadful thing happened. Mother Browneyes came running back from Wishing Wood in a terrible state, crying and groaning in distress.

"What's the matter, what's the matter?" cried the brownies.

"Oh, oh!" wept Mother Browneyes. "I was walking in the wood this morning, when who should come up but Kookle the wizard. And no sooner did he set eyes on pretty little Princess Peronel than he said: 'Ha! I will have her marry me!' And oh, brownies, whatever shall we do? He caught her up then and there and carried her off to his castle!"

"Goodness gracious! What a terrible thing!" cried all the brownies in horror. "Our little Princess with that horrid old wizard! Whatever can we do?"

Well, they decided to go at once to the castle and demand Peronel back. So they trooped off, scores of them, all feeling very angry, but frightened too in case Kookle should turn them into beetles or frogs.

They arrived at the castle, and then of course they remembered that it had no doors. They couldn't knock because there was no knocker, and they couldn't ring because there was no bell. They just stood there wondering what in the world they could do.

"Hie! Hie!" suddenly shouted Tinker, the fat little brownie. "Kookle! Kookle! If you're anywhere in the castle, just listen. Give us back Peronel at once!"

Suddenly the wizard appeared at a window and looked down at the brownies. He laughed loudly.

"Ho!" he cried. "If you want Peronel, come in and get her. Ho, ho, ho!"

"We can't!" yelled Tinker in a rage. "There are no doors!"

"Then go away!" said the wizard. "If you're not all gone by the time I count ten, I'll turn you into muffins! Ha, ha! Now – one, two, three . . ."

But by the time Kookle came to ten, there wasn't a single brownie to be seen.

They had all fled down the hill.

"We *must* do something," said Tinker. "We can't let Peronel be captured like this. But unless we find the door of the castle we can do nothing."

"But there *is* no door," said another brownie.

"There must be one that we can't see," said Tinker. "The wizard comes in and out, doesn't he? But by some kind of magic he has hidden it from our eyes. We must find out where it is. Then even if we can't see it we shall know where to find it and can turn the handle by feeling about for it."

"Well, couldn't we go to the castle tonight and feel all round the walls for the door?" said the other brownies.

So that night six brownies went creeping up to the castle. But alas for them! The wizard heard them, and turned them into kittens, so that Brownie Town was in despair to see six little kittens come running back that night instead of six brownies.

Tinker sat in his cottage and thought very hard. He did so want to rescue Peronel, for he thought she was the prettiest little Princess in all Fairyland. But he could think of no plan.

Next morning when Brownie Town awoke and drew its curtains back, it saw that snow had fallen in the night and all the countryside was white.

"Hurrah!" cried the youngsters. "Now we can build snowmen and play with snowballs."

Then Tinker suddenly had a wonderful idea. He tore out of his cottage to tell the others.

"We will build a big snowman in the field just outside the castle," he said. "The wizard will take no notice of that. But, before the moon is out, I will dress myself in a white cloak, and put on the snowman's hat. You will quickly knock down the snowman and I will take his place! Then I will stand there all night to see where the door is when the wizard comes out for his nightly walk!"

"Oh, Tinker, how clever you are!" cried the others. "That is a wonderful plan!"

"Six of you go and make the snowman now," said Tinker. "Make him about my size. Laugh and talk all the time, as if you were really playing and had forgotten all about Peronel."

So six of the brownies went to the hill on which Kookle's castle stood. The wizard peeped out of a window, but when he saw them building a snowman he took no further notice.

Before nightfall the brownies had built a nice fat snowman just about Tinker's size. They put a row of stones down his front for buttons, and tied a muffler round his neck. They put a hat with a feather on his head, and stuck a pipe in his mouth.

Then off they went down the hill to Brownie Town. Tinker had been very busy meantime making himself a long white cloak. Mother Browneyes had helped him, and together they had sewn six big black buttons down the front. Now the cloak was ready.

So, in the darkness before the moon rose, the seven brownies went silently back up the hill. They quickly knocked the snowman down, and Tinker stood in its place with his long white cloak round him.

The brownies wound the snowman's muffler round his neck, put the snowman's feathered hat on his head and stuck the pipe in his mouth. He was ready!

"Ooh!" said the brownies. "You *do* look like a snowman, Tinker! Well, good luck to you! The moon is just coming up and we must go."

They ran off down the snowy hill, and Tinker was left alone just outside the castle. He felt rather lonely and a bit frightened. Suppose the wizard guessed he wasn't a real snowman? Ooh, that would be dreadful!

The moon came up and soon Tinker could see every brick of the castle quite clearly. He stood on the hillside, hat on head, and pipe in mouth, as still as could be, his white cloak reaching down to his heels. He waited for an hour. He waited for two hours. He waited for three, and four and five. At midnight he was so cold that he was shivering.

"Oh my, I do hope the wizard won't see me shivering," thought Tinker in a fright. "But I can't stop shaking with the cold!"

Just at that moment the clock down in Brownie Town struck twelve. Tinker heard it – and at the same time he heard a voice inside the castle chanting a long string of magic words. Then he saw the door of the castle appearing! He saw it quite clearly, outlined in green flame, with a knocker and a handle, and a very big letter-box.

As Tinker watched, eyes wide open in surprise, he saw the door swing open. The wizard appeared in the opening, and Tinker hurriedly counted the number of bricks from the side of the castle to the door. His heart was thumping so loudly he was afraid the wizard would hear it.

Kookle stepped outside, and at the same moment the door disappeared, the place where it had been becoming part of the wall again. Then suddenly Kookle looked towards Tinker!

"Ha, a snowman!" said the wizard. "Stupid little brownies! How they do waste their time! I've a good mind to knock it all down!"

Tinker nearly died of fright. The wizard came right up to him and snatched the pipe out of his mouth. What Kookle meant to do next Tinker didn't know – but just at that moment a witch came sailing through the air on her broomstick.

"Hey, Kookle! It's time to join the big meeting. Come along!" she called.

In a trice the wizard leapt on to the broom with the witch and sailed off into the moonlit sky. Tinker sighed with relief, for he had been very frightened.

As soon as the wizard was out of sight he threw off his cloak and ran to the castle. He counted fifty-three bricks from the side, then felt for the door.

Almost at once he found the handle and the knocker. He turned the handle and the door swung open. He stepped into the castle and shut the door.

"Peronel! Peronel!" he cried. "Where are you?"

"Here! Here!" cried a tiny voice, far away. "Oh, who are you? Have you come to save me? I am right at the top of the castle!"

Tinker ran to the winding staircase and raced up it, two steps at a time. He was soon breathless for there were many hundreds of stairs. But up he went, and up and up, hoping with all his heart that Kookle would not return until he had rescued the Princess.

At the top of the castle was a small tower where Peronel was imprisoned. Her door was locked and bolted, but Tinker quickly drew the big bolts back, and turned the key, which the wizard had left in the lock.

The little Princess, very pale and thin, for the wizard had given her only bread and water since she refused to marry him, ran to Tinker and flung her arms round his neck.

"Oh, you dear, brave brownie!" she cried. "Thank you so much for saving me!"

"You're not saved yet!" said Tinker. "Quick, we must get out of the castle before the wizard comes back."

Down the hundreds of stairs they ran to the big door, which was easily seen from the inside of the castle. But Tinker couldn't open the door! No matter how he twisted the handle and pulled, that door wouldn't open!

For two hours he tried, but at last he gave up. Only the right magic words could open it from the inside, he realized.

"I know what we'll do!" said Tinker at last. "It isn't a very good plan, but it might work. I expect the wizard will see that the snowman is gone and guess that I am here. He will come rushing into the castle in a fearful rage. Now I've got some string here. I'll tie it from this stool to that chair over there, and when the wizard comes in it will trip him up, and perhaps we shall just have time to run out of the castle."

"Yes, that's a good plan," said Peronel. "But don't let's try to run all the way down the hill to Brownie Town, because the wizard would surely catch us. Just outside is a rabbit-hole. Sandy, a very nice bunny, lives there, and I know he would let us shelter in his burrow till the danger is past."

"That's splendid," said Tinker. He quickly tied the string across the hall just beyond the doorway. Then he and Peronel crouched down in a dark corner near the door.

Suddenly they heard the sound of an angry voice outside. It was the wizard, who had discovered the snowman's cloak on the ground.

"What's this! What's this!" he cried in a fury. "This is a trick! That snowman was a brownie, and he saw me come from the castle! Well, he can't get out. I'll catch him, yes, I will!"

The door flew open and the wizard rushed in. He caught his foot on the string and down he fell with a crash! The door began to close, but Peronel and Tinker slipped through in a flash. The Princess led the brownie to a rabbit-hole, and the two crept down it. The bunny came to meet them, and they explained to him in a whisper.

"Come this way," said Sandy. He led them to a little round room, where there was a tiny fire and a jugful of cocoa warming by it. "Help yourselves to the cocoa, and there are biscuits in that tin. I'm just going to the hillside to see what is happening. Don't be afraid. You are quite safe here."

So Tinker poured Peronel a steaming hot cup of cocoa, and gave her some sugar-biscuits. Then he helped himself, for he was hungry and cold. They sat there, warm and happy, till Sandy the rabbit came back.

"Ha!" said Sandy in glee. "That old wizard is in a dreadful temper. He bumped his head when he fell down, and hurt his knee. He tore down the hillside after you, for of course he didn't know you had come here. He couldn't find you, so he's gone back to his castle to bathe his head. I shouldn't be surprised to find that he leaves Brownie Town quite soon."

All that night the brownie and Peronel stayed with the kind rabbit. Next morning they followed Sandy down many long winding underground passages that led to the bottom of the hill. There they came out into the sunshine and said goodbye to the rabbit.

What a welcome they got in Brownie Town! How all the brownies cheered! And how pleased old Mother Browneyes was to see the Princess again! It really was a very happy morning.

Just as they were all as happy as could be, listening to Tinker's adventures, there came a big BANG! Everyone rushed out to see what was happening, and a very strange sight they saw!

Kookle the Wizard, having made up his mind to leave Brownie Town, had worked a spell on his castle. With a big BANG it had risen into the air and was now sailing away to the east, flapping two huge wings that had grown out of the walls.

"Ooh!" said all the brownies in surprise and joy. "That's the end of the old wizard! He'll never come here again! Let's give a party this afternoon to show we're happy!"

So they did, and the Princess sat next to Tinker, who was happier than he had ever been in his life before. And when Peronel presented him with a lovely gold watch for saving her, you should have heard all the brownies cheer!

The mischievous panda

The toy panda was good and quiet and kind until the afternoon when he saw Mummy putting coals on the nursery fire with the tongs.

Usually Mummy took the shovel and shovelled the coal on. But that afternoon the knobs of coal were too big for the shovel, so Mummy used the tongs. She opened the two sides of the tongs, got hold of a piece of coal, gripped it tightly, and then opened the tongs again to drop the coal on to the fire.

The toy panda was sitting by the fender, and so he saw all this very well. He hadn't known that the tongs could open and shut like that, and pick up things and let them go.

He longed to use them himself. He sat and thought about it. He gave a little giggle when he thought of himself picking up the clockwork mouse with the tongs.

"That would be a shock for the mouse!" he thought. And from that afternoon the toy panda was really very mischievous and annoying.

He picked up the tongs that night and practised opening and shutting them. Then he ran at the clockwork mouse with the tongs open.

"Here come the tongs!" he shouted. "Look out, look out!"

The clockwork mouse was most surprised to see the panda rushing at him with the tongs. He didn't even think of getting out of the way. So the panda was able to close the tongs about him and grip him tightly.

"Let me go! You're hurting!" cried the mouse. But the panda only squeezed him more tightly. Then he let him go and ran after the pink rabbit.

The rabbit was bending over the brick-box, trying to find something he had dropped there.

"Here come the tongs! Look out, look out!" shouted the panda, and in a trice they closed round the surprised rabbit. He fell on his face in the brick-box, and the panda wouldn't let him go till he had squeezed all the breath out of him.

"Stop it, Panda," said the teddy bear. "It hurts people. Don't be silly."

But the tongs seemed to have gone to the panda's head and made him quite wild. He rushed at the fat little bear and got hold of him with the tongs, too. The bear had a growl in his middle, and when he was squeezed he had to growl. So he growled and he growled and he growled, and he simply couldn't stop.

"My growl's wearing out!" he gasped. "Let me go, you unkind thing!"

The panda wouldn't let the teddy bear go till his growl had almost worn out. The bear was very angry. So was everyone, but the panda really was dangerous when he had the tongs, so nobody liked to say very much. They just kept out of his way.

But night after night he got hold of the tongs, and sooner or later he would catch somebody and squeeze them. The toys got very tired of him indeed.

The bear went to see a friend of his. This was Squiddle the pixie, who lived in the honeysuckle just outside the playroom window.

"Squiddle," said the bear, "can you do something about Panda? He seems to have gone mad lately." And he told Squiddle all about it.

"Oh yes, I think I can cure him," said Squiddle. "I'll give him an awful fright, and make him afraid to touch the tongs again."

"What will you do?" asked the bear.

"Well, you know I can make myself invisible, so that nobody can see me, don't you?" said Squiddle. "All right, then, I'll make myself invisible, and I'll hop down into the playroom tonight and go to the tongs before the panda does. And, hey presto! Just as he gets near them, those tongs will rise up and rush at him! And then they'll do quite a lot of surprising things to him that he won't like at all."

"But it will be you, really, using the tongs, and he won't see you," said the bear, and laughed.

"Oh yes, it'll be me all right," said the pixie. "And none of you will see me at all. What fun!"

Well, it really was very funny indeed. The panda, as usual, ambled off to the fender where the tongs were kept – and, to his great alarm, as soon as he got to them they stood up on end and clicked together! Then they jumped at him!

"Oooh, don't!" said Panda. But it wasn't any good saying anything. The tongs got hold of him, held him so tightly that he gasped, and then very neatly dropped him into the waste-paper basket. Plonk!

"Oooh," said the panda, horrified, and

climbed out. No toy liked to get into the waste-paper basket, in case it was emptied into the dustbin next day.

The tongs were waiting for Panda. As soon as he was out of the basket, they danced at him again, caught hold of him, and ran him over to the coal-scuttle!

Plonk! In he went among the coal. The panda couldn't bear it. He had such a nice white coat – and now it was all spotted with black.

The toys laughed. "Aha, Panda! You've had plenty of games with the tongs. You can't blame the tongs if they have a few games with *you*!"

"Oh, no, oh, please, no!" squealed the poor panda and rushed away from the coal-scuttle as soon as he was out. But the tongs were after him. And this time they tried to push him down a mouse-hole. He couldn't go, of course, because he was much too fat, but it was very painful being pushed into a hole he couldn't go down.

When at last he got away from the tongs he rushed into the toy cupboard and got under a heap of toys at the back. The bear whispered to the invisible pixie, who was holding the tongs and enjoying himself immensely. "Let him go now. He's very upset," he said.

"Where's that panda?" cried the goblin, pretending he was the tongs speaking. "Where is he? Gone! Aha, I'll be waiting for him tomorrow night. We'll have a fine game again, won't we, Panda?"

The panda shivered and shook. He didn't ever mean to go near those dreadful tongs again. And each night now he keeps as far away from the fender as he possibly can.

"He's cured," said the bear. "He's our own nice, quiet, good little panda again. Oh dear, wasn't it funny to see the tongs dancing about and rushing after him! Poor Panda!"

The little toymaker

George and Fanny were excited because Mummy had said they could go out for a picnic by themselves.

"If you cross over the road very carefully and go to the hill above the long field you should be all right," said Mummy.

So they set off, with George carrying the basket. In the basket were some egg sandwiches, two rosy apples, a small bar of chocolate, and two pieces of ginger cake. There was a bottle of lemonade as well, and George and Fanny kept thinking of the cool lemonade as they crossed the road, went through the long field and up the hill. They did feel so very thirsty!

There were ash and sycamore trees up on the hill. Already they were throwing down their seeds on the wind – ash spinners that spun in the breeze, and sycamore keys that twirled down to the ground.

George picked some up and looked at them. "Aren't they nice?" he said. "Throw some up into the air, Fanny, and see them spin in the wind to the ground. The tree is pleased to see them twirling in the wind, because then it knows that its seeds are travelling far away to grow into big new trees."

After a while the children sat down to have their lunch. They began on the egg sandwiches, but before they had taken more than a few bites they saw a most surprising sight. A very small man, not much higher than George's teddy bear at home, came walking out from behind a gorse bush. He carried two baskets with him. One was empty and one was full. The full one had sandwiches and milk in it, and the children thought that the small man must be having a picnic, just as they were.

The little man didn't see them. He had a very long white beard that he had tied neatly round his waist to keep out of the way of his feet. He wore enormous glasses on his big nose, and he had funny pointed ears and a hat that had tiny bells on. The bells tinkled as he walked. Fanny wished and wished she had a hat like that.

"What a very little man!" said Fanny. "Do you suppose he is a pixie or a brownie?"

"*Ssh!*" said George. "Don't talk. Let's watch."

So they watched. The little man walked along, humming a song – and suddenly he tripped over a root, and down he went! His full basket tipped up, and out fell his sandwiches and milk. The bottle broke. The sandwiches split open and fell into bits on the grass.

"Oh, what a pity!" cried George, and he ran at once to help.

The little man was surprised to see him. George picked him up, brushed the grass off his clothes, and looked sadly at the milk and sandwiches.

"Your picnic is no use," he said. "Come and share ours. Do!"

The small man smiled and his face lit up. He picked up his baskets and went to where the children had spread their picnic food. Soon he was sitting down chatting to them, sharing their sandwiches, cake, and chocolate. He was very pleased.

"Why was one of your baskets empty?" asked Fanny. "What were you going to put into it?"

"Ash and sycamore keys," said the small man. "There are plenty on this hill."

"Shall we help you to fill your basket?" said George. "We've eaten everything now, and Fanny and I would like to help you."

"Oh, please do," said the small man. So the three of them picked up the ash and sycamore keys, and put them neatly into the basket.

"Why do you collect these?" asked Fanny. "I would so like to know. Do you burn them or something?"

"Oh, no. I'm a toymaker and I use them for keys for my clockwork toys," said the little man. "Come home with me, if you like. I'll show you."

He took them over the top of the hill and there, under a mossy curtain, was a tiny green door set in the side of the hill. The little man pushed a sycamore key into the door and unlocked it. Inside was a tiny room, set with small furniture and a big work table.

And on the table were all kinds of toys! They were made out of hazelnut shells, acorns, chestnuts, pine cones, and all sorts of things! The small man had cleverly made bodies and heads and legs and wings, and there were the toys, very small, but very quaint and beautiful. The children stared at them in delight.

"Now, you see," said the little man, emptying out his basket of keys on to his work table. "Now, you see, all I need to do is to find keys to fit these toys, and then they can be wound up, and they will walk and run and dance. Just fit a few keys into the holes and see if you can wind up any of the toys."

In great excitement the two children fitted ash and sycamore keys into the toys, and George found one that fitted a pine-cone bird perfectly. He wound it up – and the bird danced and hopped, pecked and even flapped its funny wings. It was lovely to watch.

Soon all the toys were dancing about on the table, and the children clapped their hands. It was the funniest sight they had ever seen! They only had to fit a key to any of the toys, wind it up – and lo and behold, that toy came to life!

"I wish we hadn't got to go, but we must," said George at last. "Goodbye, little toymaker. I do love your toys."

"Choose one each!" said the little man.

So they did. Fanny chose the bird, and George chose a hedgehog made very cleverly out of a prickly chestnut-case and a piece of beech-mast. It ran, just like a real hedgehog does, when George wound it up.

And now those two toys are on their playroom mantelpiece at home, and they are so funny to watch when George and Fanny wind them up with ash and sycamore keys. I can't show you the toys – but you can go and find ash and sycamore keys in the autumn for yourself, if you like. There are plenty under the trees, spinning in the wind. Find a few, and see what good little keys they make for winding up fairy toys!

The little mouse and the squirrel

There was a little mouse who lived in a hole in a ditch. He ran about all night long, looking for titbits everywhere – and one night he went into a cottage and sniffed about for a bit of bacon or a piece of cheese.

Aha! What was this? Bacon rind, smelling fresh and delicious! The mouse ran to it and began to nibble.

But alas! It was a trap; and there came a loud rap as the trap worked, and tried to catch the little mouse. He leapt backwards, but his front foot was caught and badly hurt.

The little mouse squealed and pulled

his foot away. Then, limping badly, he hurried out of the cottage by the hole through which he had come, and went back to the wood.

His sore foot made him feel very poorly. He could not go out hunting for grain and seeds as he used to do. He was hungry and wondered if he could ask help from someone.

By his hole he saw a fat grey squirrel. The squirrel was sitting up on his hind legs, his bushy tail well in the air, nibbling at an acorn.

"Hello, Squirrel," said the mouse humbly. "Could you spare me an acorn? Or could you get me a scarlet hip from the wild-rose bramble over there? I have hurt my foot and cannot go hunting for food. I am very hungry."

"What!" cried the squirrel, in a rage. "You, a mouse, dare to ask a grey squirrel for a favour like that! Of course I shall not get food for you! Do you think I am a servant of mice? The idea of asking such a thing!"

"I do not mean to be uncivil," said the mouse. "It is only that I have hurt my foot and cannot get food."

"Then ask someone else to do your hunting for you!" said the selfish squirrel, and bounded off.

The little mouse sat at the entrance to his burrow and watched the squirrel. It was autumn and the little grey creature was storing away tiny heaps of nuts here and there, so that when he awoke for a few warm days now and then in the winter-time he could go to his hidden stores, have a feast, and then go to sleep again.

He hid some acorns behind the ivy-bark. He put some nuts under a pile of leaves in the ditch. He scraped a little hole under the roots of the oak tree and put four nuts there. He went to the hollow tree nearby and hid seven acorns. He was well prepared for lean days in the winter!

The mouse wished he could go and take some of the nuts – but he could not move far because of his sore foot. He lay in his hole and nearly starved. Then another mouse ran by, and saw the thin and hungry one.

"What's the matter?" he asked, running into the hole.

The little mouse soon told him. The other mouse listened.

"Well, you know," he said, "I would dearly love to help you, but I have a large and hungry family, and it is all I can do to find food for them. It is very scarce this year."

"I know where plenty of food is!" said the little mouse eagerly. "Get it for me, and we will all share it! Look for acorns behind the ivy-bark, and in the hollow tree. Hunt under the leaves in the ditch for nuts, and under the roots of the oak tree opposite! I saw the squirrel put some there!"

The other mouse ran off in glee. Sure enough he found nuts and acorns in plenty. He carried them one by one to his own hole, fetched the first mouse, and helped him along to the hole too. Then, with all the mouse family, the first little mouse ate in peace. Soon his leg was quite well, and he could run about happily once more.

The grey squirrel slept soundly until the month of January, when there was a warm spell. He awoke and went to find the nuts – but alas for him! However hard he looked, he could *not* find anything to eat at all! His larders were empty, each one! He went back to his tree hungry, and slept again.

Then February came, and the sun sent warm fingers into the tree where the squirrel slept soundly. Once again he awoke and came scampering down, hungry as a hunter!

He searched behind the ivy-bark – no acorns there! He hunted in the ditch – no nuts there. He looked in the hollow tree – no acorns to be seen! And last of all he put his little paw in the hole he had made beneath the roots of the oak tree. No – not a nut to be found.

He must go hungry.

"I shall starve!" he said, in fright. And then he suddenly caught sight of the little mouse, who was now plump and sleek. The squirrel called to him:

"Oh, Mouse, you are fat! Let me have a little of your food, I beg you! I am lean and hungry, and I cannot find any of the food I stored away. I must have looked in the wrong places!"

"Last autumn I asked *you* for a little food!" said the mouse, stopping. "But you said no! Why should I help *you* now?"

"You are right," said the squirrel sadly. "I treated you badly. There is no reason why you should not treat me the same."

"Wait!" said the mouse. "There *is* a reason why I should not treat you the same, Squirrel! You and I are not alike! You are selfish and greedy, but I am not. You shall share what I have!"

He brought the squirrel two nuts and an acorn. The squirrel thanked the mouse humbly, and vowed that he would repay the mouse when he found his own stores that he had hidden away.

"I was lucky this winter," said the little mouse, with a gleam in his eye. "I found four heaps of nuts and acorns – one behind the ivy-bark – one in the ditch – one in the hollow tree – and one under the roots of the oak. So I and my friends have feasted well!"

The squirrel listened. At first he was angry, but then he remembered that, after all, the mouse had let him have some food.

"So these are *my* nuts and *my* acorn!" he said. "Well – I deserved to lose them for my greed! Forgive me, Mouse! Next autumn I will store up a larder for you too!"

He kept his word, and now he and the mouse are great friends, and if you see one, you will know that the other is somewhere nearby.

The marvellous pink vase

Once upon a time Mr and Mrs Squabble went to a fair. Mr Squabble spent ten pence on the hoopla, and tried to throw wooden rings over the things spread out on a table. Mrs Squabble spent five pence, and she was very lucky. One of her rings fell right over a marvellous pink vase.

It was very tall, and had pink roses painted all the way up. Mrs Squabble was simply delighted with it. When the man gave it to her she beamed with joy.

"Isn't it lovely?" she said to Mr Squabble as she carried it home. "I wonder where I'd better put it."

Now Mr Squabble only liked vases when they were put so high up on a shelf or bookcase that he couldn't knock them over. So he made up his mind that he would say the vase would look fine on the top of the grandfather clock.

When they got home Mrs Squabble put the pink vase down on the table and looked around her living room. "Now where shall I put it?" she said. "It must be some place where everyone will see it, because it really is beautiful."

"Well, my dear, I should put it on the top of the grandfather clock," said Mr Squabble at once.

"On the top of the *clock*!" said Mrs Squabble, in surprise. "What a silly place! You never put anything on top of grandfather clocks."

"Well, why not?" asked Mr Squabble. "It would be quite a new place. I should love to see it there. Then, whenever I looked to see the time, which I do quite twenty times a day, I should see the vase. It's a marvellous place."

"Well, I don't think so," said Mrs Squabble firmly. "I shall put it on this little table here, near your armchair."

Mr Squabble looked on in horror as he watched Mrs Squabble put the vase on a rickety little table near his chair. He knew quite well that the first time he reached out for his newspaper he would knock the vase over.

"Now, my dear," he said, "that's a foolish place. Only you would think of such a silly place."

"Oh! How dare you say a thing like that!" cried Mrs Squabble. "Just because I didn't like the top of the grandfather clock!"

"Well, if you don't like that, what about putting the vase safely up there on the top of the radio?" said Mr Squabble, trying to speak in a nice, peaceful voice.

"Really, Squabble, you do think of some stupid places!" said Mrs Squabble. "Why, every time you turned on the radio, the vase would shake and might fall over."

"I don't think so," said Mr Squabble.

"Though if you turn on the radio when that dreadful woman with the screeching voice sings, the vase might jump right off in alarm."

"I'll put the vase on the mantelpiece," said Mrs Squabble. But that didn't suit Mr Squabble at all.

"I shall knock it over when I reach up for my glasses," he said.

"Clumsy person!" said Mrs Squabble.

"Indeed I'm not!" said Mr Squabble. "Why, I could walk on flower pots all around the living room and not fall off once. And that's more than you could do!"

Well, of course, that was quite enough to make Mrs Squabble fetch in twenty flower pots from the shed and stand them around the living room.

"All right!" she said. "Now we'll just see who is clumsy and who is not! You start walking on the flower pots that side, and I'll start walking on them this side. And whoever falls off first has lost, and the other one can choose where to

put the pink vase. And let me tell you *this*, Squabble – that *I* shall win without any doubt at all!"

The two of them started to walk on the upturned flower pots. They did look silly. Round the living room they went, and round and round, neither of them falling off, for they were being very, very careful.

And then the cat jumped in at the window and made Mr and Mrs Squabble jump so much that they fell off their flower pots at the same moment and fell crash against the little table.

The pink vase was there. It wobbled – it fell over – it rolled off the table – it tumbled to the floor with a bang – and it smashed into a hundred pieces!

The cat sat in a corner and washed itself. "Now they'll both know where to put the marvellous pink vase!" the cat purred to itself. "There's only one place now – and that's the dustbin!"

Peter's busy afternoon

"**M**ummy! Where are you?" cried Peter, rushing at top speed into the kitchen.

"Peter, don't make me jump like that," said his mother, almost dropping the tin of cakes she was taking out of the oven.

"Oooh, Mummy – may I have one of those buns?" said Peter at once. His mother looked at him.

"Did you post my letter for me this morning?" she asked him. Peter put his hand in his pocket and drew out a letter, going rather red as he looked at it.

"Blow – no, I didn't. Sorry, I'll post it now. Then may I have a bun?"

"No," said his mother. "Give me the

letter. I'll ask the milkman to post it. I'm afraid you can't have a bun, as you haven't even bothered to do this little thing for me."

Peter sulked. He kicked the leg of the table. "Stop doing that," said his mother. "What was it you wanted to ask me when you came rushing in, Peter?"

Peter cheered up. "Oh, Mummy –

could you give me some money, please? There are some simply wonderful pistols in the toy shop. They go BANG like anything."

"Why should I give you any money?" asked his mother, setting the buns to cool on a tray. "Why should you expect anyone to do things for you and give you things when you never, never do anything for anyone else?"

"Oh! I *do*," said Peter, indignantly.

"Did you tidy out the shed for Daddy when he asked you?" said his mother.

"No, I forgot," said Peter.

"Did you mend your little sister's brick box when you had broken the lid?" asked his mother.

"No," said Peter, sulkily.

"Did you post my letter? Did you fetch me the meat? Did you remember to shut the back gate? Did you pick up your coat from the floor?" asked his mother.

"No, I suppose I didn't," said Peter, and kicked the leg of the table again.

"Well, then – why should you expect

me to please you and hand out money to you, if you don't do anything for anyone else?" said his mother. "No, Peter. You can't have the money. I feel ashamed of you. Go away, please. I don't really feel I want to talk to you any more."

"Well, you *might*," said Peter, looking hurt. "Eileen's in bed with a cold – I do think you might let me be with you as I can't be with her."

"It isn't much of a cold," said his mother. "You *could* be with her if you wanted to. She would love you to read to her because she's too little to read herself."

"I suppose I'd better go up then," said Peter, unwillingly.

"No. She's asleep now," said his mother. "And I have asked Ronnie to come and be with her this afternoon. He's always so nice with the little ones. She won't want you."

Peter kicked his way out of the kitchen, scuffling his shoes on the floor as he went. He went and sat down in the shed, looking gloomy.

He didn't like his mother saying she didn't want him with her. He didn't like Ronnie being asked to read to Eileen. He felt left out.

Then he began to be a little more sensible. It was his own fault. He never remembered to do a single thing he was told! No wonder his mother said she didn't want to talk to him.

He kicked his heels against the box he was sitting on. He thought of Ronnie reading to Eileen. He was fond of his gentle little sister and he didn't want somebody else taking his place. He was fond of his mother, too. "Yes, I am, though nobody would think it!" he said to himself, kicking the box harder and harder. "Blow! I'd better turn over a new leaf. The thing is – can I? New leaves are jolly hard to turn over!"

When he saw Ronnie going up the stairs to play with Eileen that afternoon he felt rather upset. He must begin the leaf-turning as soon as possible! He belonged to a nice family and it wouldn't do to be the only nasty one in it. Daddy was always unselfish and generous as well as his mother.

He went to the shed and tidied it thoroughly. It looked very nice when he had finished it. Then he took out his mother's bicycle and cleaned it. It did look lovely when it was done. "And I shan't let Mummy pay me for doing it, like she did last time," he thought. "I'll do it for nothing, just to show her I'm not always selfish and forgetful."

He saw Wags the dog and gave him a good brushing. He remembered that the back gate wanted a nail under the latch to make it work properly, and he went and hammered one in. He began to have a very nice feeling inside him, indeed.

"Now what can I do for Eileen?" he thought. "I simply must do something, so that she'll know *I* was thinking of her while Ronnie was reading to her."

He went to Eileen's little garden. He knew she wanted to plant some flower seeds there. She was saving up to buy them. Her garden was full of weeds and wanted digging over.

Peter didn't like digging. He screwed up his nose and wondered if he would tackle it. Yes, he would. So he went to get a spade and a basket.

He weeded the whole of the little garden, and then he took the spade and began to dig.

It was hard work. He dug and he dug and he dug. He had to take off his coat. Then he had to take off his jersey and dig in his shirt-sleeves! Gracious, who would have thought that a little garden like that needed so much digging?

Wouldn't Eileen be pleased! My word, she'd be very, very surprised when she saw how nice her garden looked. What a pity she hadn't got enough money to buy her seeds the very next day and plant them now the garden was ready!

Peter wished he had some money, then he could buy her some. But he hadn't even a penny.

He was just digging the very last bit of all when his spade turned up something that shone. He bent down and picked it up. He rubbed the wet earth from it – and what *do* you think it was!

"A shining, silvery coin!" cried Peter. "What a find! How in the world did it get here?"

And then he remembered. "Of course! Eileen had some money on her birthday, and she lost it when she went to water her garden that evening. And it must have dropped out of her pocket then, and got buried – and here it is!"

Peter was as pleased as if it had been his own money! He raced indoors with it. He actually remembered to scrape his shoes and wipe them well. He ran up the stairs.

"Eileen! Oh, hallo, Ronnie! I say, Eileen – I was digging up your garden just now – and I found the money you lost on your birthday. Look! Now you can buy all the seeds you want – and your garden is ready to plant them in!"

"Peter! Why, how marvellous!" cried Eileen, her face going red with delight. "My own money! And what a lot of money! I'll buy my seeds tomorrow, if Mummy lets me go out. I'm much better now. Thank you, Peter, *thank* you, for doing my garden. It was most awfully kind of you!"

Daddy and Mother were told about the bit of good luck. Mother smiled at Peter. "Who cleaned my bicycle?" she said.

"I did," said Peter. "For nothing – just to make up a bit, you know, for the things I forgot."

"Who tidied the shed for me?" asked Daddy.

"I did – and that was for nothing, too," said Peter.

"Who mended the back gate?" asked

Mother. "And who brushed Wags? He looks so nice."

"Well, I did," said Peter, rubbing his nose as he always did when he felt a bit awkward. "I know I'm pretty awful most times, Mummy – but honestly, I'm turning over a new leaf at the moment. And please don't think I did it just to get that pistol, because I didn't."

"I don't think that, dear," said his mother, and she kissed him.

Now, the next day, Eileen went out with her birthday money and the money she had already saved, and bought her seeds. Then she marched off to the toy shop. Can you guess what she bought? Yes, she bought that pistol.

She walked home with it proudly. She showed it to her mother, and made it go off BANG!

Peter heard it and came rushing in. "Oh! You lucky, lucky girl, you've got the pistol I've been longing for! Did you buy it out of the birthday money?"

"Yes," said Eileen. "I had some over.

So I bought it. Isn't it fine?"

"Rather! Will you lend it to me just *some*times?" said Peter, longingly.

"No. I'll *give* it to you," said Eileen, with a laugh. "Why, I *bought* it for you, silly! *I* don't want a pistol. Here you are, Peter. If you hadn't dug my garden you wouldn't have found my birthday money, and I wouldn't have been able to buy my seeds to plant today. And I wouldn't have had any money over to buy your pistol!"

Well, what do you think of that? Peter was so pleased that he let out a tremendous whoop of joy, which made Wags jump almost out of his skin.

"Oh, *thanks*! I say, isn't it super? BANG, BANG, BANG! Oh, Mummy, does it make you jump? I promise I won't shoot it in the house."

"Thank you, Peter," said his mother. "And as you've turned over a new leaf, I can depend on your promise, can't I? Well – I'm very, very glad you got your pistol."

The flyaway broomstick

There was once a most annoying pixie called Poppo, who lived in Wobble Village on the borders of Fairyland. He was annoying because he was always borrowing things and never returning them.

"It is such a nuisance," said one small pixie to another. "That naughty Poppo borrowed my kettle yesterday, and now he says he didn't. So I have had to buy a new kettle!"

"And I had to buy a new set of dusters," complained another. "I hung mine out on the line, and Poppo came and borrowed them all without asking me. Then he said he hadn't, so I had to go out and spend all my money on some new ones."

"If only he wasn't so powerful," sighed a third. "But we daren't refuse him, or scold him, because he knows more magic than any of us."

"Yes, and do you remember how he turned little Sylfay into a worm because she told him he wasn't a borrower, he was a robber?" said the first one. "We can't do anything, you know."

But matters got so bad that the village knew they would have to do *something*. Poppo borrowed, or took without asking, all their nicest things. He would never give them back, and often said he had never had them at all. The little folk were in despair.

"I will go to the wise woman on top of Breezy Hill," said Chippy, the leader. "Perhaps she will be able to help us."

So he went off the next morning and told his tale to the old wise woman. She listened, and for a time said nothing.

"You must be careful," she said. "This Poppo is quite a powerful pixie."

"I know," sighed Chippy. "But surely, oh wise woman, you can think of some way to stop him?"

The wise woman thought again. Then she smiled. She went to a cupboard, and took out a long broom.

"I have an idea," she said. "Take this broomstick home with you, Chippy. It once belonged to a witch, and it flies in the air. There is a flyaway spell hidden in it that will take twelve people for a flight and bring them back safely. But the thirteenth flight takes it to the witch it once belonged to, and she will keep for a servant the thirteenth rider."

"Ooh!" said Chippy, frightened. "Well, what are we to do?"

"Fly it in front of Poppo's house," said the wise woman. "Let twelve pixies, one after another, have a ride, and then stop. Put it somewhere so that Poppo can borrow it – and if he doesn't fly off to the witch, then I am no wise woman!"

Chippy grinned in delight, and hurried off to Wobble Village with the fine broomstick. He whispered all about it to the others, and in great glee they went to Poppo's cottage.

"I'll have first ride," said Chippy. He sat astride the broomstick and waited. Suddenly it rose into the air, circled round the tree-tops, shot up high, and then glided gently down to the ground again.

"Fine! Fine!" cried all the watching pixies.

"Someone else can have a turn now," said Chippy. He slid off, and another pixie leapt on. Up rose the broomstick again, and away it went over the tree-tops.

When the fifth ride was being taken, Chippy saw Poppo looking out of his window. Chippy grinned. Each of the pixies had a turn, but after the twelfth ride, Chippy stopped them.

"No more," he said. "It's tea-time. We must all go home. I must take my broom into my backyard now, and use it for its proper purpose — sweeping!"

Off they all went. Poppo watched them go. He badly wanted a ride, but he wasn't going to say so. No, he would go to Chippy to ask him for the loan of his broom, saying that he wanted to sweep out his backyard.

So after tea he put on his hat and went round to Chippy's cottage. Chippy was watching for him, for he felt sure he was coming.

"Good evening, Chippy," said Poppo. "Would you be so good as to lend me a broom?"

"Ha ha! You want to ride on it!" said Chippy, pointing his finger at him.

"Indeed I don't," said Poppo, looking offended. "I want to sweep my backyard."

"Well I warn you — if you ride on it you'll be taken off to the witch who owns it!" said Chippy, who felt it would not be fair to let Poppo have the broom without a warning. "No, Poppo – I think I won't lend it to you, after all."

Poppo scowled as he went off. Chippy watched him. Soon the mean little pixie returned by the back way, creeping quietly into the backyard, where he had spied the broom. He meant to take it without permission.

He ran off with it. Chippy whistled to his friends, and they all went softly after Poppo to watch what would happen.

"I said he wasn't to borrow it, and I warned him what would happen if he rode on it," said Chippy. "It will be his own fault if he is spirited away. He said he just wanted to sweep out his backyard."

The pixies peeped over the wall. Poppo had the broom by the kitchen door. He was looking at it carefully.

"All the other pixies had a ride, so I don't see why I shouldn't, too," said

Poppo. "That warning of Chippy's was all made up – he just said it so that I shouldn't have a nice ride like the others!"

He jumped on the broomstick. At once it rose into the air. It circled three times round the tree-tops, rose very high – and then went off like a streak of lightning to the west, where the old witch lived!

"Ooh! He's gone!" cried the pixies.

So he had; and as he never came back I suppose the witch took him for her servant. He is probably there still. The pixies were delighted to be rid of him. They went to his cottage and took away all the things that Poppo had borrowed and forgotten to return.

"Good old wise woman!" said Chippy. "I'll bake her a cake this Saturday!"

He did – and she was simply delighted.